MARC BROWN

ARTHUR GOES TO CAMP

THANK YOU DON
ROBIN
SALLY & GEORGE
MELANIE

FOR LAURIE
MY FAVORITE DOCTOR

**A TRUMPET CLUB
SPECIAL EDITION**

Reprinted by arrangement with
Little, Brown and Company
Printed in the United States of America
April 1989   10 9 8 7 6 5 4 3 2 1

Published by The Trumpet Club
666 Fifth Avenue
New York, New York 10103
Copyright © 1982 by Marc Brown

The Trademark Dell® is
registered in the U.S. Patent
and Trademark Office.
ISBN: 0-440-84012-0

"I'm not going!" said Arthur.
"Arthur, you'll love camp. Think of all
the new friends you'll make," said his mother.
"I have fond memories of my own camp days,"
said Arthur's father. "Camp will teach you
about the great outdoors."
"I'm *not* going!"

Arthur was at the camp bus stop the next morning. Buster was standing with a new kid. "He's got a hundred comic books in his foot locker," squealed Buster, pointing to the Brain. Francine was there, too.
"You guys better watch out! Tent 3 is full of bats and snakes!" she yelled out the window.
"It's going to be just like school: the girls against the boys," thought Arthur.

When the bus passed Camp Horsewater,
even the girls stopped teasing.
"Look at those guys," said Buster.
"They're going to be in great shape for our
scavenger hunt. No wonder they always win!"
"That's no camp — that's a zoo," said Arthur.

Dear Mom and Dad,
I'm not at camp yet.
I'm very homesick and
I miss you very much.
Please write soon.
Love, Arthur

**Things were different at Camp Meadowcroak.
Well, at least for the girls.
"I'll do my best to make this a wonderful summer
for you," said the girls' counselor, Becky.
Even Muffy looked eager when
she pulled up in her limousine.
"Where do I plug in my air conditioner?"
she hollered.**

The boys' counselor was a different story.
"Attention, men! Line up," barked Rocky.
"Stand up straight! Suck in those guts!
I've never seen such a soft, flabby bunch.
No dessert for you men this summer!"

Muffy had brought her own dessert.
After a dinner that tasted like macaroni and fleas
and wormburgers, she opened her trunk.
The girls dug in. At bedtime Muffy discovered
the tent had no electricity.
"How will I brush my teeth?" she moaned.

The boys were too tired from all their running
and pushups to think of brushing their teeth.
They crawled under the covers.
Arthur screamed.
"Amphibians. How fascinating," said the Brain.
"No, they're frogs," said Buster.
"Just wait until we get hold of those girls,"
said Arthur.

"Forget about the frogs," said the girls. "You guys
better worry about the softball game instead!"
The girls were beating the boys at everything.
"Disgusting," said Rocky.
"I'll never live this down."

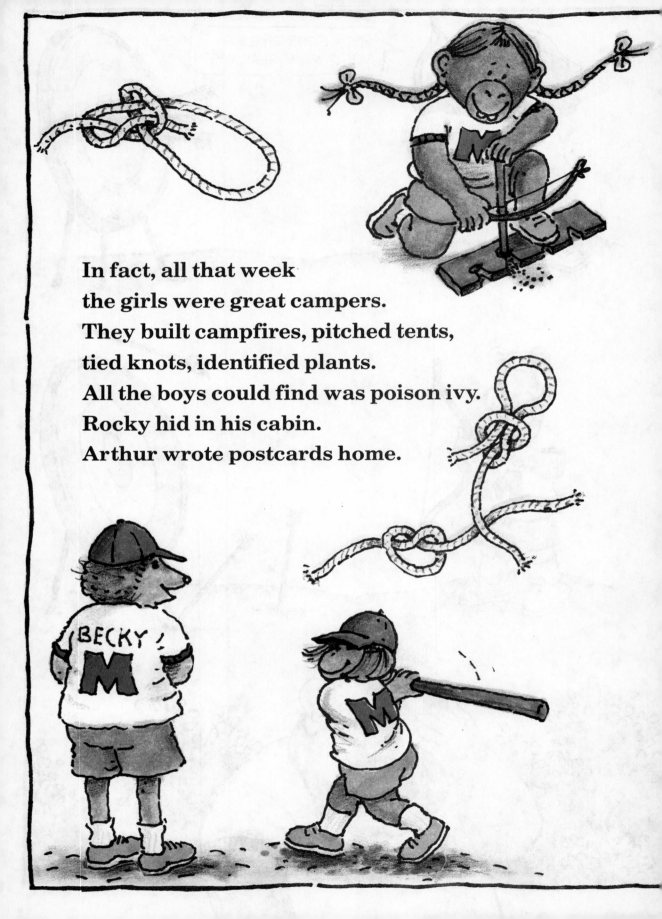

In fact, all that week
the girls were great campers.
They built campfires, pitched tents,
tied knots, identified plants.
All the boys could find was poison ivy.
Rocky hid in his cabin.
Arthur wrote postcards home.

Arthur had a lot to write about.
The frogs in his bed were bad enough,
but now really weird things were happening.
The girls thought the boys threw a smoke bomb
into their tent.
The boys thought the girls took all their clothes.

But one night everybody heard strange
noises and footsteps in the woods.
It had to be someone else.

Everyone was too scared to tell ghost stories.
"We have to do something," said the Brain.
"Let's stand watch tonight and find out
what's going on."

"So that's it! Camp Horsewater!"
whispered Buster. "They've been trying
to scare us all along."
"Don't worry, we'll fix them tomorrow
at the scavenger hunt," said the Brain.
"I've got a plan. But we'll need the girls' help."
Arthur had a plan, too.
He decided to run away.

Dear Mom and Dad,
I desided not to wait
for you to come and
get me.
I think I can remember
how to get home.
Love, Arthur

The next morning Becky read
the list of things to find.
"And be back at sunset," she said.
The Brain nudged Francine.
"Time for phase one of The Plan," he whispered.
"Watch out for bears — the woods are
full of them," she yelled to the Horsewater kids.
They just laughed.
Nobody noticed Arthur sneaking away.

Everybody was in the woods looking for things.
Strange noises started coming from the bushes.
Suddenly a huge, furry animal
burst from the underbrush.
"A bear!!" hollered Muffy and Buster and Francine,
trying not to giggle.

When the Meadowcroak team
started hunting again, the bear helped, too.
"How can you wear this coat, Muffy?" the Brain's
voice floated out from the fur. "It's so hot."
"It's never too hot for mink." Muffy grinned.
"Our plan really worked, but we still haven't found a
flashlight. And has anyone seen Arthur?" said Buster.
"It doesn't matter if the Horsewater team
never comes down from the trees. We can't win
if we don't have everything," groaned Francine.

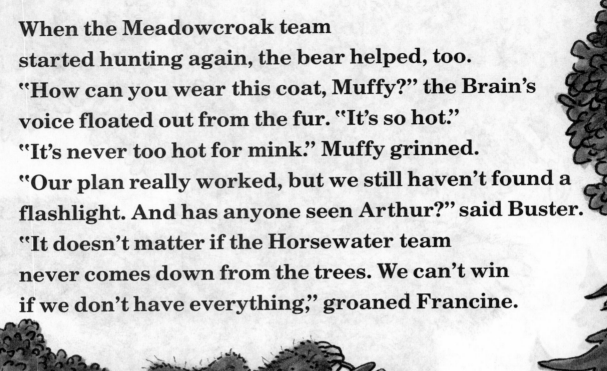

Meanwhile, it was getting dark
and Arthur was lost.
He heard strange noises.
Were they footsteps?
Arthur reached into his
backpack for his flashlight.
He snapped it on.

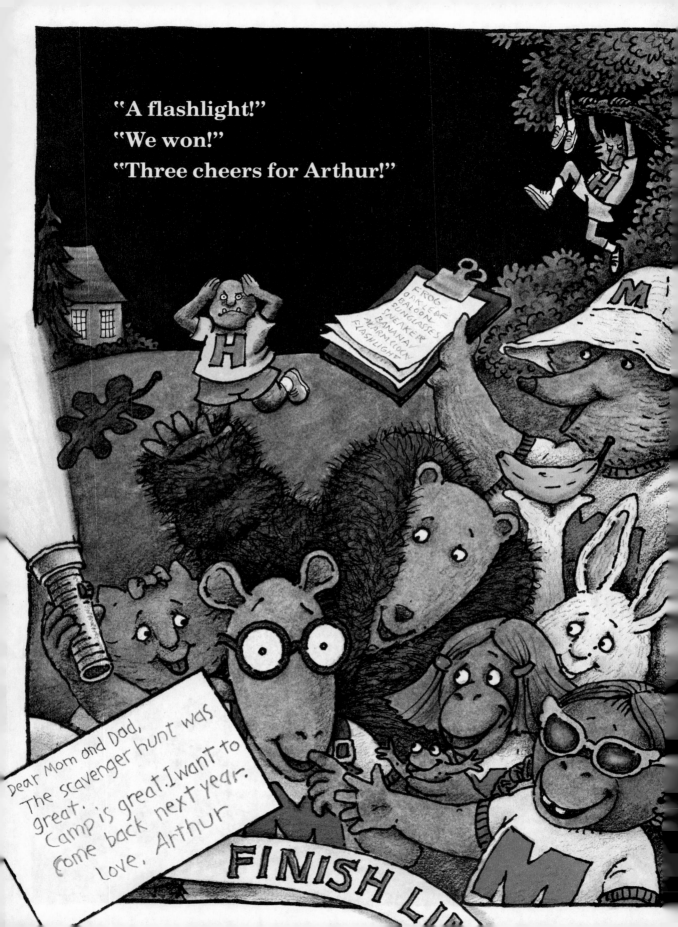